Abby and the Seahorse

learn

chemistry

To order additional copies of this book, contact:
Xlibris
844-714-8691
www.Xlibris.com
Orders@Xlibris.com

ISBN: 978-1-6698-0893-0 (sc)
ISBN: 978-1-6698-0894-7 (e)

Print information available on the last page

Rev. date: 04/08/2022

Grateful acknowledgements:

Dr. Locke

Dr. Johnston

Calli Baldack

Wikipedia. Org. Viewed
in January 17, 2022

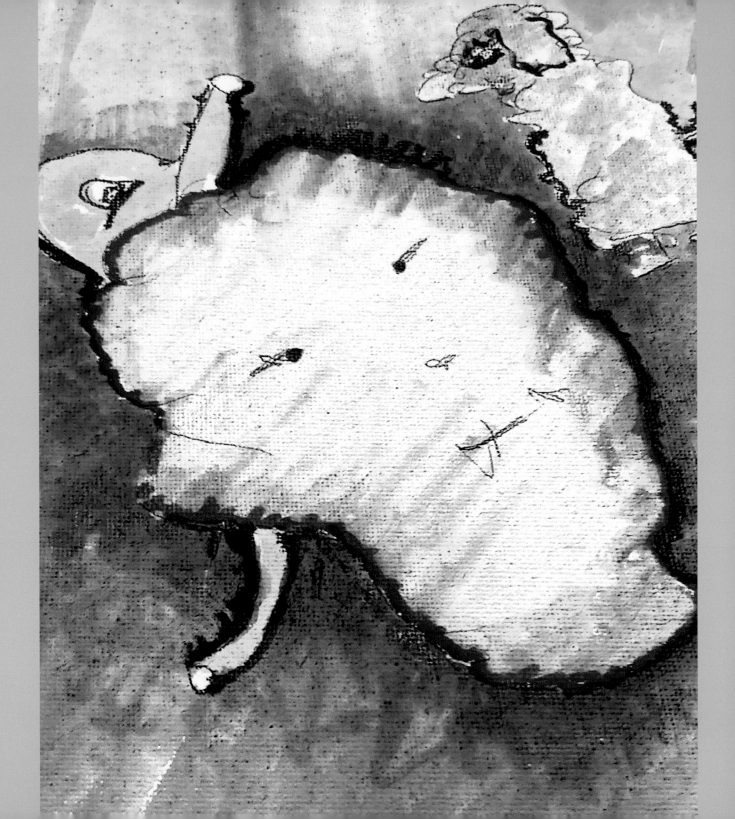

The face starts talking and asks the seahorse if they have a cat friend. The cat is his favorite pet. They say they do and will bring the cat next time.

Abby asks the Face what the coordinates are where the face lives. The face says 35.9375 N and 14. 3754 E.

Next Abby and the seahorse visit
a different part of the world.
The penguins ask Abby and the
seahorse how they got there.

Sailing says the detective ducks.

A combination reaction has occurred with the detective ducks. A + B = AB.

A replacement reaction has occurred as Abby has replaced the seahorse. ΛBCD splits to AC + BD.

The first sail comes to life and is curious what the Ph of seawater is.

The detective ducks say it
should be around 8.1.

The second sail says what

are we made of?

The detective ducks say different woven materials including canvas and polyester cloth.

The third sail comes to life and asks the detective ducks what is the chemical symbol for water. The seahorse says H_2O.

The boat comes to life and asks
the detective ducks what can
be done to avoid rusting?

The detective ducks say wash
with water after each use.

Next they go out to California to help put out the wildfires.

Just like the ground is the work surface for fire fighter this is the work surface of a cell.

Then they go out to the Pyramids. Just like the atom is a unit of measurement so is the pyramid inch.

Lastly, they go to Mount Everest.
Just like the molecule is a unit of
measurement so are rock formations.

Printed in the United States
by Baker & Taylor Publisher Services